Rugrats™

WHERE THE SHARKS ARE

by Duncan Maxfield
illustrated by George Ulrich

SCHOLASTIC INC.
New York Toronto London Auckland Sydney

ISBN 0-590-68325-X

12 11 10   2 3/0

Printed in the U.S.A.   23

First Scholastic printing, April 1998

"Are the children ready?" Didi asked Stu as she slipped into the driver's seat.

"Yes, they are," responded Stu. "Sea Park, here we come!"

Tommy and Chuckie were strapped into their car seats. They weren't sure what Sea Park was, but they were sure they were ready.

As Didi drove, Stu read from the brochure. "It says here that visiting Sea Park is like entering an underwater world. Visitors meet face-to-face some of the most interesting and exotic animals from the sea."

"What kind of animals?" asked Didi.

"It's a long list," responded Stu. "Let's see, eels, sea turtles, barracudas, sea horses, dolphins, sharks . . . hey, Deed, I have a great idea! Why don't we buy aquariums for Tommy and Chuckie so they can create 'underwater worlds' of their own."

"That's not a bad idea, Stu," said Didi. "Let's buy what we need at the park."

"Did you hear that?" Chuckie asked Tommy, suddenly afraid. "I don't wanna take a shark home!"

"Aw, come on, Chuckie! It might be fun to have aquarrums," said Tommy.

"Here we are!" announced Didi as they drove up to the Sea Park entrance.

In front of them was a huge sign in the shape of a shark.

"Wow!" said Tommy. "Look at that picture! It's the neatest thing I ever saw!"

"I have a bad feeling about this," said Chuckie gloomily.

Didi and Stu pushed Tommy and Chuckie in their strollers through the park entrance into the first exhibit area. All around them swam schools of fish.

Nearby, a huge silvery fish drifted slowly. Tiny fish with rainbow-colored stripes darted among tall strips of wavy seaweed.

"See, Chuckie, these fish wouldn't be too scary to have at home," said Tommy.

"I dunno," Chuckie responded.

They came up to a signpost with arrows pointing in different directions.

"Uh-oh," said Chuckie.

"What's the matter?" asked Tommy.

"Sharks!" gasped Chuckie, pointing to one of the signs.

"Stu, let's have a look at those sea otters," said Didi.

Chuckie breathed a sigh of relief. "Tommy, what are sea odders?"

"I guess those are," said Tommy. They stopped in front of an exhibit where four long furry animals were frolicking in the water. "It did a somersault!" he said.

"These might not be too bad to have at home!" said Chuckie.

"Let's head for the sea horses next," suggested Stu. "I've always been fascinated by them."

"Sea horses?" said Chuckie to Tommy. "How would I fit one of those in my room?"

"I dunno," said Tommy. "Maybe you'd have to get a really big aquarrum."

"Here we are," said Didi. "Aren't they a hoot?"

The babies peered up at the sea horses as they bobbed around in the water.

"They don't look like horses!" said Tommy to Chuckie. "They're kinda cute."

"Yeah, I guess they wouldn't be too bad," said Chuckie, doubtfully.

"What good timing," said Stu, as they approached the Sea Park arena. "They're about to start the dolphin show."

"What are dobbins? They don't sound friendly," said Chuckie to Tommy, nervously.

"Ah, come on! Don't be a baby!" said Tommy. "It might be fun!"

They found seats up front. Everyone clapped when the trainer walked out to the pool area.

"Welcome, kids! Does everybody out there want to see the dolphins jump?" the trainer asked the audience. The audience cheered. The dolphins began swimming in circles around the pool, faster and faster.

"All right then . . . get ready. Here we go. One, two, three!" The dolphins leaped into the air at the same time.

"Look!" Tommy cried. He elbowed Chuckie, who had covered his eyes with his hands.

"But, Tommy," said Chuckie, "where would we put them?"

After exiting the arena, Stu and Didi walked up to an ice-cream vendor to buy snacks for the babies.

"This looks like it might be interesting," said Chuckie as he wandered into a nearby building.

"Uh, Chuckie, I think you should know . . ." Tommy began.

Chuckie walked up to a glass tank and found himself face-to-face with a long row of sharp, shiny teeth.

"Shark!" shouted Chuckie.

"Chuckie, are you okay?" said Tommy as he ran up to the tank. The shark immediately turned around and swam away. "Thanks, Tommy, you scared him away!" said Chuckie.

"There you children are," said Didi as she rushed up to them. "It's time to go home now. But first we'll head over to the Sea Park gift shop."

"But, Tommy, I don't wanna take a shark home!" Chuckie wailed.

A few minutes later they left the gift shop.

"These goldfish are great," said Tommy.

"Yeah," said Chuckie happily. "*These* I can fit in my room."

"You know, Stu," said Didi behind them. "I think we should visit the circus when it comes to town. The children would really enjoy seeing the lions and elephants."

"Oh, no," groaned Chuckie. "Not again!"